Paul Simon
Greatest Hits, Etc.

Paul Simon
Greatest Hits, Etc.

bbi · quick fox

Produced by Steve Rauch
Special thanks to Ian Hoblyn
Book and cover design by Ira Friedlander
Front cover photograph by Marie Cosindas
Back cover photograph by Edie Baskin

Photo Credits

Peter Simon	8 (top), 23, 27, 28–29
Dagmar	8 (bottom)
Edie Baskin	8, 13, 14, 18, 19, 24–25
NBC	11
Adrian Lewis	9
Bill Pierce	16–17
Allen Tannenbaum	20

Distributed to the book trade by Quick Fox, A Division of Music Sales
Corporation, 33 West 60th Street, New York, N.Y. 10023.

Distributed to the music trade by Big Bells Incorporated, 33 Hovey Avenue, Trenton, N.J. 08610.

International Standard Book Number: 0–8256–3916–6
Library of Congress Catalog Card Number: 77–93716

CONTENTS

THEMES AND VARIATIONS

1. Where the Songs Come From

What we have here is a long way from a conventional greatest-hits collection. Undoubtedly, there were those who thought it should be one, but Paul Simon had another idea: a collection that would represent not only his most commercially successful songs but also his artistic favorites and some hint of his forthcoming work.

However, eight of these songs have been Top 20 hits in the past five years. (Simon has also had two other Top 20 records, "My Little Town" and "Gone at Last," which are not included here.) It is hard to think of another artist who could match that much commercial success with the great artistic stature Paul Simon's work enjoys. (It is also possible, even as I write, that a ninth hit is being created: "Slip Slidin' Away" has just been released as a single.)

Those songs provide a neat focus for this collection because as hits, burrowed and pounded into the public consciousness, they lead dual existences: as events, on record, and here, as songs written by one of our era's major popular composers. For instance, who can think of "My Little Town" (one of Simon's unanthologized hits) without calling to mind first that it marked Simon's being rejoined by Garfunkel for the first time since *Bridge Over Troubled Water*.

Yet to think of the song in that way—or at least in that way alone—ignores its other, obvious virtues: the ominous bass notes from the piano that signal the theme; the easy syncopation leading through a desolate lyric landscape; the mood transition, from despair to defiance, signaled by piano and drum; the striking horn arrangement, which makes those famous harmonies so much richer. It's as sophisticated a

piece of popular tune-smithing as anyone has assembled. To see it nostalgically, or as a vehicle for gossip and speculation, is wasteful.

Not that such attachments are always bad things. They are what make us care about songs and think more than twice about them. But beyond curiosity, there remains music, the heart of the matter. In retrospect, what is striking about Paul Simon's solo work — in marked distinction to his earlier music with Simon and Garfunkel — is its diversity of musical style, which ranges from the reggae of "Mother and Child Reunion" to the gospel of "Loves Me Like a Rock" to the jazz-tinged "Something So Right." In addition, of course, there is much more maturity, both in the musical structure of these songs and in their lyrical themes, in Simon's solo work.

Consider the growth from "Bridge Over Troubled Water," the final Simon and Garfunkel hit, to "Mother and Child Reunion," Simon's first on his own. "Bridge" is a splendid statement, a hymn that spoke for and to a couple of generations and the gaps between them. Yet there is a finality about its innocent spirit; it is the logical culmination of a musical style — itself quite sophisticated in pop terms — which had evolved since "The Sounds of Silence," its bitter opposite.

"Mother and Child Reunion" was illogical; it broke the pattern, which was part of its point. The keynote of its eccentricity, of course, was its rhythmic structure, particularly because it was the first reggae hit by a white American artist. Here is a case where the record dominates our perception of the song almost completely; it is almost impossible to imagine this song without the shuffling Jamaican rhythm accents. But its lyric is also drastically different

from anything Simon had previously written. Addressed to a mythical daughter, it is quite clearly a meditation on the ironies and tragedies of mortality.

It may be indicative of Simon's working process that the song is a result of both serendipitous word-play and a deeply personal experience. "Know where the words come from?" he asked *Rolling Stone* interviewer Jon Landau in 1972, shortly after his first solo LP was released. "I was eating in a Chinese restaurant. There was a dish called 'Mother and Child Reunion.' It's chicken and eggs. And I said, 'Oh, I love that title. I gotta use that one.' "

But the rest of the lyric came from something less trivial. "Last summer," he told Landau, "we had a dog that was run over and killed, and we loved this dog. It was the first death I had ever experienced personally. Nobody in my family died that I felt that. But I felt this loss — one minute there, next minute gone . . . I don't know what the connection was. Some emotional connection. It didn't matter to me what it was. I just knew it was there."

This happens to be a strikingly adult way of looking at such an event. It is typical of the increasingly mature perspective that marks Paul Simon's solo work. And the growth lyrically has been accompanied by — is, in fact, secondary to — a simultaneous and perhaps greater increase in musical sophistication. Almost alone among his peers from the Sixties, Simon has managed to find a way to grow up in his music while retaining his connection with those who responded to early songs that were angrier and less complex.

" 'Mother and Child Reunion,' for example, is not a song that Simon and Garfunkel would have done," Simon commented to Landau. "It's possible

Although some of his early work earned him a reputation as something of a Pollyanna, Simon's ''messages'' have always been fairly tough-minded, and they have grown more so as he has matured artistically.

that they might have. But it wouldn't have been the same. I don't know if I would have been so inclined in that direction. For me, it was a chance to back out and gamble."

If Simon and Garfunkel seemed a safe bet by the end, one can see every step of Simon's solo career as a calculated risk. Another way to look at it is to think of Simon's evolving standards of excellence; those who know him will affirm that he's not simply painstaking about music but also his own severest critic. If the solo career was a bit of a long shot (at least in elementary commercial terms) there were gambles within that bet: experimentation with non-pop commercial genres (jazz included), with song-writing styles, compositional techniques, and even a shift away from guitar as the central instrument of his work, to the piano, which offers more diverse melodic opportunities.

It is both the bane and the delight of Simon's music that it has never seemed risky or experimental. Though these songs have connected heavily with great numbers of listeners, it would be a gross mistake to call them conventional in any way. Simon has never honored the boundaries of musical style in any event. Unlike most post-Elvis writers, he has as much respect for George Gershwin as Jerry Leiber and Mike Stoller. But unlike most sophisticated pop songwriters, he knows rock and uses it effectively and meaningfully. Thus, working (in recordings and performances) with non-pop musicians such as jazz violinist Stephane Grappelli, the gospel singers the Dixie Hummingbirds or the Peruvian instrumentalists Los Incas and Urubamba is a natural outgrowth of his writing.

These things became immediately apparent in 1972 with the release of the *Paul Simon* album, his first as a

solo artist. Simon and Garfunkel's music was highly polished, but on *Paul Simon* he went for feel — and got it. The sound was diverse: "Mother and Child Reunion" was recorded with reggae musicians in Jamaica, "Duncan" with Los Incas in Paris, "Hobo's Blues" with the gypsy master musician Grappelli. Even the more "standard" instrumentation had a more biting edge than any of the Simon and Garfunkel songs.

In addition, Simon was beginning to feel his way into more overtly personal lyrical material. "Everything Put Together Falls Apart," "Run That Body Down," and "Paranoia Blues" were statements about health, mental and physical, that passed easily from the personal to the generational. "Peace Like a River," "Armistice Day," and elements of some others were social commentaries much more direct than any Simon had previously recorded.

For all of that, however, Simon is far from grim, even in his earliest solo songs. In fact, one of the characteristics of his style is a kind of epigrammatic, elusive wit. "Mother and Child Reunion" even has its ironic couplet: "I know they say let it be/But it just don't work out that way." Simon's humor is rarely so referential, but it's often just that dry (and like most dry humor, some listeners miss it completely). "Me and Julio Down by the School-yard," on the other hand, is super-ficially only a joke, almost a break into slapstick. But Simon, of course, didn't mean the song as only a harmless, whimsical novelty. Although he told Landau that it was "pure confection," there was also something else going on. What *was* it that "mama saw/ It was against the law"? "I have no idea what it is," Simon said. "Something sexual is what I imagine; when I say 'something,' I never bothered to figure out what it was. Didn't make

any difference to me. First of all, I think it's funny to sing — 'Me and Julio.' It's very funny to me. And when I started to sing 'Me and Julio,' I started to laugh and that's when I decided to make the song called 'Me and Julio,' otherwise I wouldn't have made it."

On record, "Me and Julio" is nothing more than a simple guitar strum, with the addition of Airto

9

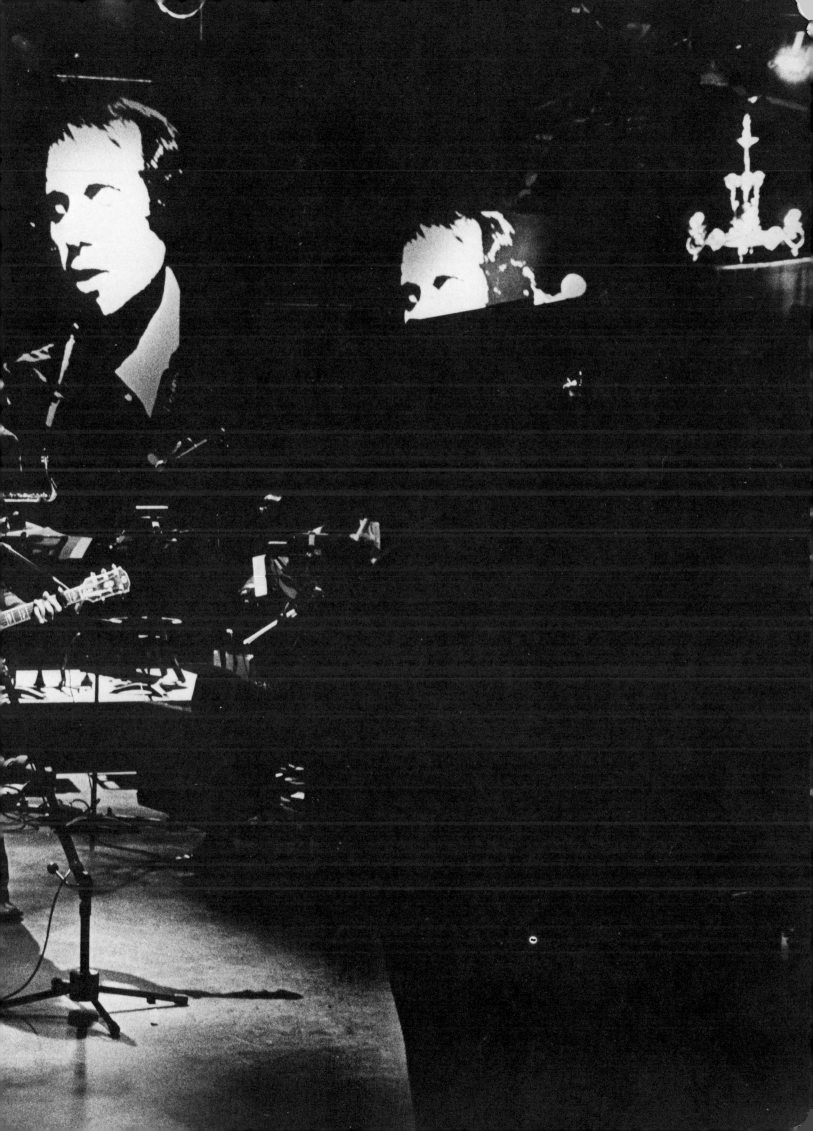

2. Freedom

Moreira's percussion and punctuated by electric bass. But the acoustic guitars are effervescent, a perfect mood for this sort of thing. The words manage to turn a subject Simon has taken with great seriousness on this album — the radical-left politics of the Sixties — into a grand, broad farce, an inside joke he shares with his fans. The couplet about the radical priest is a perfect encapsulation of the era's benighted spirit. (On the original *Paul Simon* album, the song is heard in sharp emotional counterpoint, because it is followed by the much more somber "Peace Like a River," which deals with the same sort of protests. The latter uses a similarly skeletal arrangement to much different — even opposite — effect.)

There is a third kind of song on the *Paul Simon* album, best exemplified by "Papa Hobo" and "Duncan" (the latter is included here). "Duncan" is a song of character and experience, almost of adventure. The presentation, Simon's guitar and voice backed by Los Incas, whose charango and percussion add a marvelous bottom to the sound, plays against Lincoln Duncan's story of a boy come down from Canada's Maritime Provinces to lose his virginity in the big city. (There is a parallel here with Simon and Garfunkel's hit "The Boxer," in which another naive young man comes to the city, though with more disastrous consequences.)

"Duncan" is actually a pretty droll story, almost a shaggy-dog tale, a characteristic that's enhanced by the way Simon sings certain lines: "I was born in the boredom and the chowder," "Holes in my confidence," "I'd like to hock it," and the single word "survival" which stretches until it nearly breaks. It gives an early indication of the freedom Paul would enjoy as a solo vocalist.

That freedom was enhanced by Simon's second album, *There Goes Rhymin' Simon*. This is Simon's brightest and most openly rocking collection, perhaps because so much of it was recorded with the Muscle Shoals Rhythm Section, one of the great soul bands. In any case, it seems less dominated by ballads than any of his other works, much more upbeat, although the record does contain "St. Judy's Comet," "Something So Right," "American Tune," and a couple of others that are distinctly "down" in mood. It is true, though, that aside from "American Tune," *There Goes Rhymin' Simon*'s best-known songs are open and fairly happy ones, at least on the surface: "Kodachrome," "Loves Me Like a Rock," "Was a Sunny Day," and even "One Man's Ceiling Is Another Man's Floor" lend *There Goes Rhymin' Simon* a kind of optimistic feel — though there's tension lurking beneath the surface, as shown by the songs from that album included here.

"Kodachrome" is similar to "Me and Julio" in its juxtaposition of mood and content. It is perhaps the funkiest number Simon has ever done, and the arrangement works overtime to keep the pace. Guitars jangle, the keyboard rattles along — there's a terrific slur in the midst of the second chorus — and it rushes to a climax that's next to ragtime in its jollity, barely modified Jerry Lee Lewis in its intensity. But Simon keeps things so light on top that it's easy to miss the biting ironies of the lyric. For me, at least, "Kodachrome," which opens *There Goes Rhymin' Simon,* is the clearest line of demarcation between his old and new artistic identities. Musically, it resides in the center of his new work; its use of diverse elements, and the specific

elements with which it works, are rather typical of the rest of the LP and Simon's solo approach in general. More importantly, its tone and lyric set a theme of disillusionment that would haunt almost all of the songs in the *Rhymin'* set and much of the next one.

The details of "Kodachrome" aren't as significant as its sensibility and the ways in which that sensibility shifts and changes. Still, if there is a key line in Paul Simon's solo work, "everything looks worse in black and white" might be the one, dismissing as it does the false Technicolor of our fantasies, while insisting on the narrower spectrum of the lives we really lead.

What this means in practice can be seen more clearly by comparing *Rhymin' Simon*'s "American Tune" with Simon and Garfunkel's "America." (Both, of course, were written by Paul alone.) As similar in mood as they are, the differences between the songs are drastic. Though each manages to sum up a specific emotional and cultural era, the similarities end there.

"America," released on the 1968 LP *Bookends,* seems today a masquerade. Only something so elementally naive could maintain such pretensions to totally cool irony (of course, this is one of the reasons it is such an apt relic of that age). Simon's eye for detail is perfect already — the "cigarettes and Mrs. Wagner's pies" of the first verse leap out of the song, a verbal hook — and the bus ride is the ideal metaphor for the rambling, displaced Sixties. Indeed, in retrospect, the musical arrangement is also surprisingly sophisticated. Although it's all acoustic guitar and harmony on the surface, the drums are strong, the swirling organ is a perfect folk-rock ploy, and there is a sinuous soprano sax part lurking in the bridge. All of this builds to the final two lines, which are meant to evoke the spirit of the era:

> *Counting the cars on the New Jersey Turnpike*
> *They've all come to search for America*

The problem, perhaps, lies as much with the time as with the tune — certainly, "America" is less smug,. more palatable than the Pollyanna platitudes of the bushels of hippie prophecies and polemics then making the rounds. But it's inadequate to the real reach of the issue; there's something more important than car counting to the insistence of searching for the heart of a land when we barely know the first thing about ourselves.

"American Tune" repeats a good deal of this ground but in a much more aware perspective. There are moments when it totters on the edge of bitterness and gall, but it rights itself with simple respect and devotion: There is an American ideal — and Simon knows it well — that brings him back to the theme.

The arrangement of "American Tune" is modest, a simple acoustic guitar duet over electric bass building in an orchestrated crescendo, but that humility enhances the convictions of the singing. Simon is wistful, patient, weary, but refuses to surrender, though he acknowledges every problem. In the bridge, when the strings emerge, he dreams a dream of death and (strangely?) reassurance. He sees the Statue of Liberty ("sailing away from me"), thinks back on all of us, "coming to this land on a ship they called the *Mayflower* . . . a ship that sailed the moon" and concludes with sentiments that aren't so far removed from but are considerably less confident than what he'd felt six years before:

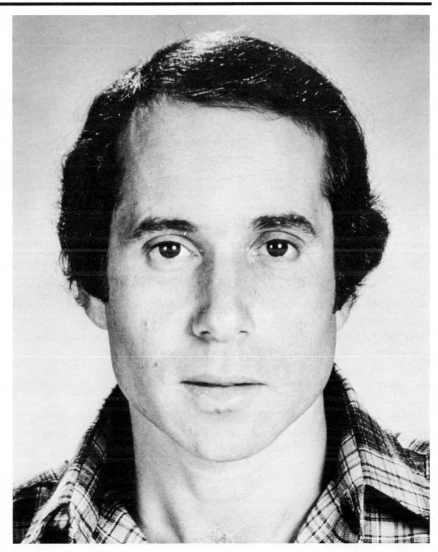

> *Ah but it's all right, it's all right, it's all right*
> *You can't be forever blessed*
> *But tomorrow's another working day and I'm just trying to get my rest*
> *Just trying to get some rest.*

The use, in both of these songs, of the strikingly unlikely, even jarring, lyric detail is a prime characteristic of Simon's writing style. "[Simon] has a theory about lyrics," wrote Paul Cowan in *Rolling Stone* in 1976. "That listeners can't absorb line after line of rich poetry, that songs should consist of simple spoken English backed by a single powerful image that makes them magic. He's reading poets like W. S. Merwin, Edwin Muir, and Ted Hughes to learn what he can from their art."

Cowan also pointed out that Simon's "urbanity and his interest in musical techniques led him to identify with the tradition represented by George Gershwin." Speaking with Paul shortly thereafter, we found ourselves in a long discussion about the Tin Pan Alley songwriters of the past

and how he felt an intimate connection with them, although the root of his experience was still in the musical style of his generation — rock and roll.

This stream of Simon's work comes to a head in this collection's most startling song, "Something So Right." It is the most obviously sophisticated piece of music on the set, with greater range and eclecticism than even any of the songs on *Still Crazy After All These Years*.

The first and most important thing about "Something So Right" is that it swings — which is to say its parts have an ease and naturalness that brings them together with dramatic force and absolutely no evidence of strain. A good deal of this is thanks to the wonderful rhythm section, particularly drummer Grady Tate, who pushes the song through its gliding paces with just the right touch.

The arrangement is eventually a spectacular one, but it opens with a kind of interplay between acoustic and electric guitars (Simon's plus David Spinozza's and Alexander Gafa's). This time, though, there's a jazz tinge to it, some of the ambiance of Wes Montgomery in the lightness and mobility of the picking. That feeling is heightened by the electric piano, which fills in around and underneath the guitars and voice.

A good part of the swinging quality of the tune is Simon's voice; it's huskier than normal, almost veering into blues. Here his phrasing, always fine, is superb. Listen to what he does with the chorus's "it's apt to confuse" and "it's such an unusual sight," wringing the irony from them. With the second verse, however, this basic arrangement is supplemented with vibes and one of the best pop string arrangements that Quincy Jones has ever done. Tate picks up the pace nicely, and suddenly, however exotic

14

> **66 I started to follow musical examples, not sociological examples. I realized that how you dressed or how you looked or what you said wasn't as important as whether you had the musical goods. 99**

all this complexity makes it seem, this is also a typical Simon arrangement. Unlike other pop arrangers, he uses strings and other instruments to heighten what's going on in the rhythm section, rather than overwhelm or disguise it.

There is something of the magic of Cole Porter or Noel Coward — not to mention Gershwin — in this structure, and the same influences show up in the lyrics. The song might be called confessional, in the way that many of Joni Mitchell's recent songs are, but it also has a wry touch of humor almost no one since those great Tin Pan Alley writers has used so deftly. "When something goes wrong," Simon boasts, "I'm the first to admit it. The first to admit it and the last one to know." The phrasing comes out of an almost cynical speech pattern, but it's a big part of this song's "rightness."

Yet it would be a mistake to place Simon wholly within the Gershwin – Porter structure. His influences are not only more diverse than the Brill Building; he understands very well what things influenced the Tin Pan Alley writers (even the great ones) to write as they did. In a way, "Take Me to the Mardi Gras" is a bit of homage to the place where, it sometimes seems, every musical sound in America has its origins, a tribute to both New Orleans rhythm and blues and the city's traditional jazz (not quite what is known today as "Dixieland" but close to it). "Mardi Gras" is, I think, one of the most deeply felt songs Simon has written. There's a kind of emotion everyone who loves American music inevitably associates with New Orleans and the multitudes of bands and musicians who parade on Mardi Gras Day.

The Muscle Shoals rhythm section immediately must have picked up this spirit of tribute; their playing has never

been more sensitive, particularly the bassist-drummer combination of David Hood and the brilliant Roger Hawkins. In addition, the voices Simon chose to accompany him are perfect, particularly the falsetto solo of Reverend Claude Jeter. But the most wonderful moment comes at the very end as the Onward Brass Band comes in with the purity of a century-long tradition of New Orleans music-making.

The Onward Brass Band, in a way, offers a connection between both "Take Me to the Mardi Gras" and "Something So Right," as jazz-influenced compositions, and between "Mardi Gras" and "Loves Me Like a Rock," as gospel-inflected ones. "Loves Me Like a Rock," an enormous hit and the final selection from *Rhymin' Simon* in this collection, is another example of the eclecticism and diversity of Simon's influences and his willingness to expose them. "I like other kinds of music," he had told Landau. "The amazing thing is that this country is so provincial. Americans know American music. You go to France. They know a lot of kinds of music. You go to Japan and they know a lot of indigenous popular music." The point is well taken but might be expanded: Americans also generally know very little about the various kinds of American music.

"Loves Me Like a Rock" is a secular gospel song; on the album, Simon is backed by one of the more distinctive black gospel groups, the Dixie Hummingbirds. Simon has toured, meanwhile, with another gospel group, the Jessy Dixon Singers, who appear with him on the *Rhymin' Simon* album. "Loves Me Like a Rock" is a bit of whimsy, with more than a shade of deviltry in its spirit. Of all Paul Simon's songs, it is closest to the rock and roll and rhythm and blues of the 1950s.

15

Simon is critically regarded as something of an auteur, and like the movies of the auteur film directors, his records have been taken to be revealing of his personality.

3. Departures

"**G**one at Last" was something of a key to the third Simon solo album, *Still Crazy After All These Years*. In one way, that album is the pinnacle of Simon's style; yet in another it represents a sharp departure for his work. The important point is the shift in composition, away from the guitar-dominated structures he'd used for almost all of his previous songs and toward the piano, the very essence of gospel (no accident that Ray Charles and Aretha Franklin are also very great pianists), as well as the central compositional instrument of both traditional popular and European classical music.

That fundamental difference — a keyboard at the root of so many of the compositions rather than a guitar — had begun with parts of *There Goes Rhymin' Simon*, but it became much more pronounced on *Still Crazy*. And it explains why most of *Still Crazy After All These Years* sounds somehow very different from everything else he has done.

That change occurred for a variety of reasons, some very pragmatic, some completely artistic. The most practical was that Simon had a physical problem, a calcium deposit on one of the fingers of his left hand, which causes it to become discolored and swollen at frequent intervals. As a result he began to look upon the piano as an important composing instrument, which in part was simply a preparation for the future.

Perhaps more significantly, Simon had begun to study musical theory, for which the piano is really the only instrument that will do. For example, he told Cowan that the music on *Still Crazy* begins with the question "What is a diminished chord?" (He told me later that each song uses every note in an octave.) But the problem he posed was perhaps less important than the fact that he was now capable of posing more challenging ones. "I don't think it matters what question you start with," he told Cowan. "As long as you start off with a question, it's going to lead to something interesting."

Rock and roll is basically guitar-based music (as Chuck Berry, Elvis Presley, the Beatles and Dylan's is), though there are important strains of piano-dominated influence, notably in New Orleans rhythm and blues, a genre that Simon had also employed on "Take Me to The Mardi Gras." But the piano alone is the central instrument of American pop tradition, from Gershwin and Berlin through Hoagy Carmichael and Cole Porter (and even Duke Ellington) to the most interesting pop melodists of the post-rock and roll age: Simon, Randy Newman, Carole King, Stevie Wonder, and, in a more obviously traditional way, Burt Bacharach. Part of what Simon has done with his solo albums is help erase the gulf between that pop tradition and rock and roll, without trivializing or patronizing either.

He explained to Cowan why he felt the change was essential. "I started to follow musical examples, not sociological examples. I realized that how you dressed or how you looked or what you said wasn't as important as whether you had the musical goods.

"I certainly see George Gershwin as somebody to measure against. Leonard Bernstein is somebody to measure against. Which is not to say that I aspire to write songs like Leonard Bernstein. But there was an excellence they achieved that was right for their time. I wouldn't do that. It wouldn't come out that way." (Not insignificantly, though, Simon's next project will probably be a musical drama rather than a simple LP, which is another way of linking his experience with the richness of the older pop tradition.)

So, in a very real sense, *Still Crazy After All These Years* was an experimental album. That it was a successful experiment — one that contained four hit singles and sold millions of copies — doesn't detract from the risk of the venture but enhances its stature. It was an essential step. Simon's art and emotive resources are now fully mature — in a word, adult — which is something that rock and roll can never be, though the spirit of that unruly music infuses much of the best of his new music. In incorporating both the pre- and post-Presley styles in his compositions, Simon helps set the stage for a new, more broadly based American music.

If so, *Still Crazy's* songs are a very significant bit of transition. In any case, taken as a group or individually, they are the very best — the richest, most complex, most deeply felt — that Simon has written. This was obscured when the album was released, by a variety of factors: The changes in composing style lent the album an unfamiliar tone that threw many listeners off the mark; the success of the album dispelled the thought of any reanalysis; the album has a constant, almost mordant, preoccupation with the dissolution of sexual relationships. I think, though, that if these songs will last, they will last less because they are some kind of personal statement about the quixotic nature of trying to maintain a relationship in this turbulent time than because of the quality of their music, which is as it should be.

Of the tunes contained in this collection, the biting ''50 Ways to Leave Your Lover'' has become the most notorious, because its lyric idea is so compelling, as lists always are. (If you

want to get technical about it, the song details only five anyway.)

"50 Ways" is a keen reminder that Simon is also a first-class lyricist and not without a sharp wit. He sings the verses with almost disaffected resignation — a man admitting defeat because he has to, not because he wants to — which allows the animation of the chorus, which otherwise might sound vicious. A large part of the appeal is in the ominous, almost military drum flourishes that set the tone and pace — music to march (out) to, I guess. This is a classically understated Simon arrangement — percus-

sion and voice are almost all we hear, but what sets them up are the guitar and organ lines which for the most part are hidden away, deemphasized in the mix.

"Still Crazy After All These Years" may be the oddest thing anyone has ever recorded with the Muscle Shoals rhythm section. Roger Hawkins, ordinarily the funkiest of drummers, taps along quietly here, as does the ordinarily extroverted pianist Barry Beckett. These are jazz elements, but played by R & B musicians, an example of the way Simon sets up challenges for his session players, insuring against formula performances. "Still Crazy" might be a form of jazz-rock — Beckett's electric piano part owes more than a bit to Chick Corea — and Simon's phrasing, which is at its most splendid, is also closer to jazz than rock or even pop. His vocal is loud, clear, even brave; it cost him something to sing these lines:

I'm not the kind of man
Who tends to socialize
I seem to lean on
Old familiar ways
And I ain't no fool for love songs
That whisper in my ears
Still crazy after all these years

© 1974 Paul Simon

I have perhaps overemphasized Paul Simon's maturity in this essay — clearly, this song feels a lot less confident about it than that. But it seems to me that maybe that is just the ultimate evidence of the truth — that the fight against the silly excesses of adolescence is never completely won. Don't all of us fear we'll do some damage one fine day? But then the agony of Mike Brecker's sax solo, arising in the bridge amidst the strings and flutes like a behemoth, tells that story well enough.

"Have a Good Time" is almost the opposite side of the "Still Crazy" coin. It has an air of ironic resignation, not about depression or despair but about happiness, a rather quirky subject for fatalism. Taking this song at face value would perhaps be the biggest mistake of all, but once again Simon has struck a common nerve: What to do about the embarrassing facts that haunt more than a few of his (and our) white middle-class privileges? The answer isn't to renounce one's station in life, obviously. Better, as the singer suggests, to grin and bear it, know the limitations of material advantage and . . . what the hell, have a good time.

With songs like this, and "Some Folks' Lives Roll Easy," Simon moves closer than ever to folk wisdom and farther than ever from folk music. "Have a Good Time" is a singular mixture of elements no one but Simon would put together in quite this way: the jazz guitarist Joe Beck played off against rocker Hugh McCracken; his own voice playing off the chorus sung by the great R & B writer Valerie Simpson, which lends a hint of Motown and late 1950s girl-group records; David Mathews' ensemble horn arrangement played against Phil Woods's wonderful sax solo at the end, which evokes everything Simon has been trying to say.

"I Do It for Your Love," on the other hand, reveals Simon's unmatched mastery of understatement. As critic Janet Maslin has pointed out, "One extraordinarily deft thing about this last album is its use of delicate accents — a change of tense in 'I Do It for Your Love,' a martial drum in '50 Ways to Leave Your Lover' — to flesh out ideas Simon's natural reticence prevents him from articulating in their entirety."

Not many rock lyrics come on like

20

poetry, much less make effective use of poetic technique, despite what they're teaching in schools these days. "I Do It for Your Love" uses exactly the kind of elusive symbolic imagery one associates with poetic imagery to perfect the vision of a love affair gone sour:

Found a rug
In an old junk shop
And I brought it home to you
Along the way the colors ran
The orange bled the blue

© 1975 Paul Simon

It is not surprising, then, that Simon felt confident enough with "Still Crazy After All These Years" to introduce the written lyrics of "My Little Town" with a quotation from Ted Hughes's poem "Two Legends."

Simon's reticence is not merely contained in the words he appends to his music. It would be a mistake to say that his music lacks dramatic force — the arrangement of "My Little Town" has as much as any popular single of the Seventies — but his songs do usually lack melodrama, the staple of the Top 40 airwaves. "I Do It for Your Love," like "Something So Right," carries this penchant for ellipsis to an extreme: It says more by quickly sketching a scene than we could learn from another artist's full-scale portrait. Ken Asher's piano and Bob James's string arrangement are the most noticeably exciting things about it, creating an easy, free-flowing groove, but hidden underneath is a swinging vocal chorus that helps Simon turn in one of the finest singing performances of his career. This is just the sort of love-song singing Paul McCartney has popularized — but McCartney has never used an arrangement half so sophisticated to support it. "I Do It for Your Love" may be a love song, but it is a long way from silly.

This anthology begins with Paul Simon's first new work since *Still Crazy After All These Years*. Following that album's release Simon did a concert tour, a couple of appearances as host of NBC's *Saturday Night Live,* a benefit performance at Madison Square Garden for the New York Public Library, and had a bit part in Woody Allen's film *Annie Hall.* (He also produced a few tracks on singer-writer Libby Titus's debut album, one of which, "Kansas City," affirms his brilliance as a horn arranger.)

During the summer of 1977 Simon was occupied with two projects. One was his first solo TV special (Simon and Garfunkel had done one in the late Sixties), which he co-produced with his good friend Lorne Michaels (who also produces *Saturday Night Live*). That special, shown on NBC in the fall, featured Simon in more than just the usual variety-show context. A script was devised that gave Paul — aided by such guests as Art Garfunkel, Eric Idle, Lily Tomlin, Chevy Chase, Chuck Grodin, and the dancer Twyla Tharp — focus for his comedic and dramatic talents. In effect, Simon and Michaels created a sixty-minute special about the making of a special.

During this period Simon also began gathering strength and material for his next major musical project. During the summer he often retreated to his beach home to prepare a project he has never publicly described. About all that is known is that it is the score for an unidentified movie whose other ingredients haven't even been hinted at.

Columbia Records released an anthology album, *Paul Simon's Greatest Hits,* in October. As the album's release date approached it occurred to Paul that he had several songs — written during the summer — that were ready to be heard. The result was that the single, "Slip Slidin' Away," which opens this set, and one other new song, "Stranded in a Limousine," also included on the album, turned the release of the album into a pop-music event. While I'm writing this before the album's release, it seems obvious that "Slip Slidin' Away" belongs in any collection of Paul Simon's work. In my opinion, at least, the song ranks immediately with his classics.

On the other hand, it would be futile to try to gauge the quality or direction of Simon's first full-fledged film score from only two songs, however successful. (The Simon score for *The Graduate,* of course, included only one song — "Mrs. Robinson" — that had not been previously released.) Certainly, neither "Slip Slidin' Away" nor "Stranded in a Limousine" reveals any basic departure from the body of Simon's work. Stylistically and thematically their concerns are of a piece with much of the rest of this collection.

In any event, the test of a soundtrack is its effectiveness as a whole and on the screen. The significance of Paul Simon's composing a soundtrack for a motion picture is the opportunity it gives him to expand his base: to work in a genre where the limitations of time are not as severe as on popular records and to work in a self-consciously integrated medium.

Each of Simon's previous albums has a cohesive point of view, of course. This is true both musically and in terms of lyrical preoccupation, though the two can finally be separated only as a matter of convenience. A film score, however, naturally demands an even firmer grasp of both sorts of theme and perhaps an even deeper integration of them.

21

Of the two new songs included in this collection, "Stranded in a Limousine" is by far the lighter, both musically and verbally. It is built around a rolling rock piano riff and a sharply syncopated rhythm pattern, both of which link it emotionally to the gospel-flavored "Gone at Last" and "Loves Me Like a Rock." But though the piano stomps just as hard, the pace is less frenetic and Simon's droll singing lends him a cool distance from the action.

From the beginning this song again has a jazz flavor. The introductory piano passages show this most overtly — a shade of McCoy Tyner even creeps in — and the feeling is abetted by the maracas that shake the song into life. This is continued by the riffing horns that first appear midway through the song. These horns are used slightly differently than they have been on Simon's other LPs, more like pop jazz than the R & B accents Simon has usually chosen. In a musical way, anyhow, "Stranded in a Limousine" is one of Simon's most soulful songs.

It is undercut, though, by the drollery of the vocal. A good deal of the time — particularly on the "wah-wah-wah" of the chorus — Simon seems to be singing for the pure joy of it.

The subject matter of "Stranded in a Limousine" is, finally, something of a mystery. In some degree, it is a character sketch. Like most lyricists, Simon generally works with types (one might even say archetypes) rather than attempting to develop character through accumulated detail, in a literary sense. While this is still true here (perhaps inevitably), the key to the song seems to be that everything happens in relation to the central character: "the mean individual." No one except him acts; others are only capable of reaction. This is another function of the droll singing — Simon

wants the character to seem "mean" but not sinister.

On the other hand, I don't think that what Simon is actually saying here is subject to direct analysis. Outside of the narrative context for which it was initially conceived, the song defies rationalization. Any interpretation would be misguided; what's more important is that the song is joyous, that Simon enjoys singing it, and we enjoy hearing him do so.

But this raises an important ancillary issue. Simon is critically regarded as something of an auteur, and like the movies of the auteur film directors, his records have been taken to be revealing of his personality. There is some logic in this presumption. Beyond that, it's also true that Simon has used autobiographical details in some of his songs (especially in his early work with Simon and Garfunkel, but even as late as *Paul Simon,* such details are fairly common). What is mistaken is the common tendency to draw the conclusions that Simon's songs — or those of any intensely personal musical artist — are somehow autobiographical.

This attitude is self-limiting and, in the last analysis, distinctly anti-art. No artist lives in a vacuum, and inevitably elements of every artist's life will become part of the detail — or the overriding spirit — of his work. This is as true of the painter's garret as it is of the successful rock artist's limousine; the problem is that the latter is much more visible. But to claim that this is finally the subject matter of the work — much less, as some would, that it constitutes the deepest meaning of the artist's efforts — is simply ridiculous and misunderstands what art, especially personal art, is all about.

In the same sense that no artist can avoid leaving the tracks of his daily life in his work, there would be no point in making art if only to reiterate what one is already living. Great art *is*

inevitably tied to the life of the artist, but to the interior life — his or her deepest desires and aspirations, or even just fantasies — not the more mundane leavings. If this were not true, any reasonably intelligent person might become a major creative force. So, although Paul Simon may make reference to real people, events and objects in his day-to-day world, these are not the fundamental subjects of his songs. Of course, the lives of artists are fascinating to us, but that ought not to be true because of a voyeuristic approach to their work. On the contrary, what we know of an artist's day-to-day existence should be used to expand our understanding of what compelled him to create the alternatives and commentary he has invented. It is insulting to treat anyone's work as a method of "reading" them, and it is not at all the proper subject of critical analysis of art.

This is all worth saying at such length here — not that it hasn't been said before — because "Slip Slidin' Away" does have such an intensely personal approach. In one of its key verses a father views his sleeping son and then must leave the house where the child rests. It is an intensely moving moment, not so much because it has an analogue in the life of the artist but because it speaks so directly to an experience so many of us know.

"Slip Slidin' Away" is an immediate Simon classic first of all because it is based on a guitar-derived melody that evokes the classic songs, not only of his solo career but even of his earliest Simon and Garfunkel albums. The mood is set by the acoustic guitar, electric bass and light drums strongly associated with the folk-rock period, and it's entrancing, subtly punctuated not only by the rhythm section but also by a quiet electric piano.

But the real story is in the singing. Simon, backed by the Oak Ridge Boys (the first time he has used a white or country-style gospel group), uses his vocal vulnerability to express weariness just this side of resignation. Simon's voice often takes on a youthful quality in songs like this with a hint of innocence of even naïveté. It is a voice he often reserves for his greatest songs.

But this time the innocence is informed by new experience. It would be a mistake to say that "Slip Slidin' Away" is a song of disillusionment, but it is brutally frank about the limits — spiritual and otherwise — of modern life.

The lyrical style is epigrammatic. Although the title is more modest, "Slip Slidin' Away" is in fact related to Simon's "state of the nation" songs, in which he attempts to catch a collective mood of sense of purpose. (Other examples include not just "America" and "American Tune" but also "Peace Like a River," "Loves Me Like a Rock," and even such very early Simon and Garfunkel recordings as "Sounds of Silence" and "Homeward Bound.") These are not attempts to gauge actual current events — what could be duller than a *song* about Watergate or the Carter presidency? — but attempts to assess the national spirit. And in that sense, which is perhaps the most important of all, Paul Simon is occasionally a true writer of spirituals.

For now, the problem is to try to measure optimism against lassitude. In one verse of "Slip Slidin' Away," Simon captures the latter with a certain precision:

She said, a good day, ain't got
*   no rain*
She said, a bad day's when I lie
*   in bed*
and think of things that might
*   have been*

Hope is harder to pin down, and not only because it is harder to find. Although some of his early work earned him a reputation as something of a Pollyanna, Simon's "messages" have always been fairly tough-minded, and they have grown more so as he has matured artistically. "Slip Slidin' Away," however, is his first song in many years to rely on overtly religious imagery. In the opening verse the man wears his passion "like a thorny crown." And the resolution is nothing less than cosmic:

God only knows
God makes his plan
The information's unavailable
*   to the mortal man*
We're working our jobs
Collect our pay
Believe we're gliding down the
*   highway*
When in fact we're slip sliding
*   away*

© 1977 Paul Simon

The point, once again, is not that Simon has become some sort of religious convert. It is another measure of his eclecticism that theological imagery is as available to his work as spiritual music. And so what might have been a hopelessly fatalistic and resigned piece offers us some hope: We have our place, we do what we're supposed to do, as best we can, and everything else will turn out, as best *it* can.

If Paul Simon's solo work, up to this point, has been a matter of personal growth, which connects so deeply with so many of us because of its parallels with our own struggle to reach maturity without sacrificing the most important values and ideals of our adolescence, then "Slip Slidin' Away" is the most fitting conclusion to this collection. For its message is not that we have won or lost but that

we are winning and losing. That in the best sense, despite the awful ennui of the era, we have remained alive and well. This is a small enough concern, but one of the reasons that "Slip Sidin' Away" touches so many listeners so deeply is that small reassurances are precisely what we need right now.

One of the nice things about Paul Simon is that he understands things like that.

With this collection Paul Simon has reached the culmination of the first phase of his solo career. He has reached every goal he could have set for himself. Commercially, he has equaled the success of Simon and Garfunkel. Artistically, there is no question that he has surpassed his early songs, both in the quality of the writing and the skill with which they have been recorded.

With Simon we confront an artist whose future has an almost limitless potential. The final question remains: What will he do next? And based on what he has already done, one hesitates to venture too many guesses.

We know some of it already. Paul Simon will write a film score. "Slip Slidin' Away" and "Stranded in a Limousine" are an indication of it. We know that he has studied classical music and music theory for several years. We know that he has begun to focus his writing around the piano rather than the guitar.

I can imagine Paul Simon going on to do many things. He might, if he wanted, have a crack at writing some modern version of *Porgy and Bess* or *Rhapsody in Blue,* a full-scale merger of pop and classical traditions which no writer of the rock generation has yet managed to pull off successfully. More likely he will find a new form, even if he has to invent it. Quite clearly, though, judging from his interest in film and dramatic presentation and his

recent production attempt, he is interested in breaking past the limitations of writing for himself alone. Once more we may find Paul Simon working in collaboration with others: arranging, producing, composing, adapting his musical vision to fit other forms and perhaps finding other artists who can sing songs he couldn't do himself, something he has not attempted since the break-up of Simon and Garfunkel.

Or maybe — and again this is not only possible; it is even likely — he will do something other than any of that. One hesitates to predict what any artist will do with his future. And if anything is made clear by the work we have at hand, it ought to be that Paul Simon is an artist of a very high order. All we can say for certain is that whatever happens, you and I and millions of others will find ourselves listening with great pleasure.

References

N Y Post p17 My 26 '73 por
N Y Times II p15+ F 27 '72 por
N Y Times Mag p48 O 13 '68 pors
New Yorker 48:32+ Ap 29 '72
Rolling Stone p36+ My 28 '70 pors
Time 99:36 Ja 31 '72 por
Ewen, David. Popular American Composers, First Supplement (1972)
Shaw, Arnold. The Rock Revolution (1969)

BIOGRAPHY

"I love my own music," Paul Simon once remarked. "I can work on my music, or sit and play the guitar all night, and I love it because it's me and I'm making it all up." Often hailed as the foremost composer of "contemporary *lieder*," Simon writes music and lyrics that transcend generational and cultural differences. Five of his compositions — among them the pop classic "Bridge Over Troubled Water" — have been played on the air more than 1,000,000 times, making him the most frequently heard composer of the post-Beatle years. In the mid-1960s the combination of Simon's meditative lyrics and Art Garfunkel's expressive voice sold millions of records. Each of Simon and Garfunkel's seven albums earned a Gold Record, and *Bridge Over Troubled Water*, their last joint release, won an unprecedented six Grammy awards in 1970. As a solo performer, Simon has continued to enjoy critical acclaim for his sensitivity, imagination, and versatility.

The son of Louis and Belle Simon, Paul Simon was born on October 13, 1942, in Newark, New Jersey. His father, a bass violinist, was a radio station staff musician who eventually taught graduate courses in education at a branch of the City University of New York; his mother was an elementary school teacher. His father is now retired. Simon grew up in Forest Hills, New York, a middle-class residential neighborhood in the New York City borough of Queens, where he attended the local public schools. He met Art Garfunkel when both boys were rehearsing for the school's sixth-grade graduation play, *Alice in Wonderland*, in which Simon portrayed the White Rabbit and Garfunkel the Cheshire Cat.

After graduating from high school, Simon enrolled at Queens College to study English literature. He recalled his undergraduate days for Susan Szekely in an interview for the New York *Post* (June 7, 1966): "My life dates back to . . . when I was nineteen. That was my year of change. . . . I was in my second year of college, a lit major, I had started to read. It was then that I started going on different paths from other people." Equipped with a B.A. degree, Simon entered Brooklyn Law School, because "it seemed the thing to do," as he explained to one interviewer, but after about six unhappy months he dropped out to pursue a career in music.

From the beginning of their joint careers, Simon and Garfunkel performed regularly in concert, before young audiences who warmed to their musicianship and collegiate casualness. Avoiding the orgiastic acrobatics of such hard-rock groups as the Rolling Stones, they were always, in the catchword of the 1960s, cool.

Because of diverging careers (Garfunkel had taken up acting) and conflicting musical tastes, Simon and Garfunkel formally dissolved their professional partnership in 1970. "It ended, and I sort of didn't want to be a partner," Simon explained to Jan Hodenfield in an interview for the New York *Post* (May 26, 1973). "I didn't want to be always half of something. . . . I think we were both in agreement that the end had come because it was too hard after it had been easy."

Simon's first solo album, a cosmopolitan collection of jazz, reggae, and rock, was released in 1972. Titled simply *Paul Simon*, it was prepared over a ten-month period in recording studios in the United States, France, and Jamaica and showcased some of the world's most popular musicians. Stephane Grappelli, the famous jazz violinist of the 1940s, played on two of the cuts, "Hobo's Blues" and

"Duncan"; Stephen Grossman, the bottleneck guitarist, collaborated on "Paranoia Blues"; and Jamaican reggae musicians added the happy, syncopated reggae beat to "Mother and Child Reunion." It sold an impressive 2,000,000 copies throughout the world.

With his next album, the singer-songwriter earned a Grammy nomination for the best LP of 1973. Less cerebral and more upbeat than *Paul Simon, There Goes Rhymin' Simon* includes the successful single "Loves Me Like a Rock," a gospel-rock number, and "American Tune," *Rolling Stone's* pick as song of the year. Enthusiastically received by the record-buying public and by critics alike, the album certified Simon's position as one of the most significant producers of contemporary American music. To coincide with the release of the album in the spring of 1973, Simon launched an eleven-city tour that culminated in London, where he played to three packed houses at the Albert Hall. Onstage he was backed by Jessy Dixon and the Dixon Singers, a gospel-singing group, by Urubamba, a South American group formerly known as Los Incas, and occasionally by his brother, guitarist Eddie Simon. In his London *Observer* "Pop" column of June 10, 1973, Tony Palmer praised Simon's music as a "celebration, both personal and universal, of the happiness that life can bring." *Live Rhymin,'* released in 1974, includes selections from his concert performances.

A short, broad-shouldered, boyish-looking man, Paul Simon stands five feet five inches tall and has dark brown hair and brown eyes. An intensely private man, Simon rarely grants interviews. "I don't want to be known, except for my work," he once told a reporter. "They've got no right to know about me, except for my songs."

DISCOGRAPHY *

Tom & Jerry:

Hey, Schoolgirl
(Big Records; released 11/5,7)

Simon & Garfunkel:

Wednesday Morning, 3 AM
(CS 9049; released 10/10/64)
You Can Tell the World
Last Night I Had the Strangest Dream
Bleecker Street
Sparrow
Benedictus
The Sounds of Silence
He Was My Brother
Peggy-O
Go Tell It on the Mountain
The Sun Is Burning
The Times They Are A-Changin'
Wednesday Morning, 3 AM

Sounds of Silence
(CS 9269; released 1/17/66)
The Sounds of Silence
Leaves That Are Green
Blessed
Kathy's Song
Somewhere They Can't Find Me
Angie
Richard Cory
A Most Peculiar Man
April Come She Will
We've Got a Groovey Thing Goin'
I Am a Rock

Parsley, Sage, Rosemary and Thyme
(CS 9363; released 10/10/66)
Scarborough Fair/Canticle
Patterns
Cloudy
Homeward Bound
The Big Bright Green Pleasure Machine
The 59th Street Bridge Song
   (Feelin' Groovy)
The Dangling Conversation
Flowers Never Bend with the Rainfall
A Simple Desultory Philippic
   (Or How I Was Robert McNamara'd into
   Submission)
For Emily, Whenever I May Find Her
A Poem on the Underground Wall
7 O'Clock News/Silent Night

The Graduate (Soundtrack)
(OS 3180; released 2/21/68)
The Sounds of Silence
Singleman Party Foxtrot
Mrs. Robinson
   (Version I as heard in the movie)
Sunporch Cha-cha-cha
Scarborough Fair/Canticle (Interlude)
On the Strip
April Come She Will

The Folks
Scarborough Fair/Canticle
A Great Effect
The Big Bright Green Pleasure Machine
Whew
Mrs. Robinson
   (Version 2 as heard in the movie)

Bookends
(KCS 9529; released 4/3/68)
Bookends Theme
Save the Life of My Child
America
Overs
Voices of Old People
Old Friends
Bookends Theme
Fakin' It
Punky's Dilemma
Mrs. Robinson
A Hazy Shade of Winter
At the Zoo

Bridge over Troubled Water
(KCS 9914; released 1/28/70)
Bridge over Troubled Water
El Condor Pasa
Cecilia
Keep the Customer Satisfied
So Long, Frank Lloyd Wright
The Boxer
Baby Driver
The Only Living Boy in New York
Why Don't You Write Me
Bye Bye Love
Song for the Asking

Greatest Hits
(KC 31350; released 6/14/72)
Bridge over Troubled Water
Mrs. Robinson
The Sounds of Silence
The Boxer
The 59th Street Bridge Song
   (Feelin' Groovy)
Scarborough Fair/Canticle
I Am a Rock
Kathy's Song
Cecilia
America
Bookends
Homeward Bound
El Condor Pasa (If I Could)
For Emily, Whenever I May Find Her

Paul Simon:

Paul Simon
(KC 30750; released 1/5/72)
Mother and Child Reunion
Duncan
Everything Put Together Falls Apart
Run That Body Down
Armistice Day

Me and Julio Down by the School Yard
Peace like a River
Papa Hobo
Hobo's Blues
Paranoia Blues
Congratulations

There Goes Rhymin' Simon
(KC 32280; released 5/11/73)
American Tune
Kodachrome
Take Me to the Mardi Gras
One Man's Ceiling is Another Man's Floor
Something So Right
Tenderness
Loves Me Like a Rock
St. Judy's Comet
Learn How To Fall
Was a Sunny Day

Live Rhymin'
(PC 32855; released 3/1/74)
The Sounds of Silence
Loves Me Like a Rock
Me and Julio Down by the School Yard
Duncan
Mother and Child Reunion
The Boxer
Bridge over Troubled Water
America
Homeward Bound
Jesus Is the Answer
American Tune
El Condor Pasa

Still Crazy After All These Years
(PC 33540; released 9/75)
Still Crazy After All These Years
My Little Town
I Do It for Your Love
50 Ways To Leave Your Lover
Night Game
Gone at Last
Some Folks' Lives Roll Easy
Have a Good Time
You're Kind
Silent Eyes

Paul Simon ● Greatest Hits, Etc.
(JC 35032; released 11/77)
Slip Slidin' Away
Stranded in a Limousine
Still Crazy After All These Years
Have a Good Time
Duncan
Me and Julio Down by the School Yard
Something So Right
Kodachrome
I Do It For Your Love
50 Ways to Leave Your Lover
American Tune
Mother and Child Reunion
Loves Me Like a Rock
Take Me to the Mardi Gras

Slip Slidin' Away

Words and Music by
PAUL SIMON

way,   slip slid - in' a - way._____   You know the

near - er your des - ti - na - tion the more ___ you're slip slid - in' a - way. _____

And I know a fa - ther ___ who had a son. _

_____ He longed to tell him all the rea - sons for the things he'd done.   He came a

Stranded in a Limousine

Words and Music by
PAUL SIMON

He was a mean in-di-

Then ev - 'ry - bod - y came _____

D. S. 𝄋 al Coda ⊕

Coda

night.

The mean in-di-vid-u-al had

van-ished in the black of night.

The

mean in-di-vid-u-al had van-ished in the black of night.

Instrumental

44

Have a Good Time

Words and Music by
PAUL SIMON

Moderately, with a Blues feeling

Tacet.

Yes - ter - day it was my birth - day; I hung one more year___ on the line.___
noi - a strikes deep in the heart - land, but I think it's all___ o - ver - done.___
laugh - ing my way to dis - as - ter; may - be my race___ has been run.___

I should be de - pressed;___ my life's___ a mess, but I'm
Ex - ag - ger - at - ing this,___ ex - ag - ger - at - ing that; they
May - be I'm blind___ to the fate of man - kind, but

Have a good time, _____ have a good time, _____

_____ have a good time, _____

have a good time. _____ Par - a May - be I'm___

D. S. al Coda

keep it that way, _and we'll all_ have a good time, _____

have a good time, _____ have a good time, _____

_____ have a good time. _____ Have a good time, _____

Duncan

Words and Music by
PAUL SIMON

Moderately slow and steady

1. Coup-le in the next___ room bound to win a prize,___ They've been
go-in' at it all___ night___ long, Well, I'm tryin' to get some sleep, but these
mo-tel walls are cheap, Lin-coln Dun-can is___ my name and here's my

song, _____ here's my song.

2. My fath-er was a fish-er-man, my ma-ma was a fish-er-man's friend, And

I was born in the bore-dom and the chow-der, So

when I reached my prime, I left my home in the Mar-i-times, _____

Headed down the turnpike for New England, __ sweet New England.

Instrumental solo

3. Holes in my confidence, __ holes in the knees of my jeans, I's

5. Just lat - er on the ver - y same night when I

crept to her tent with a flash - light,__ And my long years of in - no - cence

end - ed,_____ Well, she took me to__ the woods, say - in',

"Here comes some-thin' and it feels so good!" And just like a dog___ I was be-

friend - ed,___ I was be - friend - ed.

6. Oh, oh,_____ what a night, oh, what a gar-den of de-light, Ev-en

now that sweet mem - o - ry ling-ers, I was

play - in' my gui - tar, ___ ly - ing un - der - neath the stars, ___ Just

thank - in' the Lord for my fin - gers, ___ for my fin - gers.

Fade out

Still Crazy After All These Years

Words and Music by
PAUL SIMON

Me and Julio Down by the Schoolyard

Words and Music by
PAUL SIMON

Moderately bright

The ma-ma pa-ja - ma rolled _____ out of bed, and she ran to the po - lice sta - tion, When the pa-pa found out, he be-gan to shout, _____ and he start-ed the in-ves-ti-ga-tion.

Mother and Child Reunion

Words and Music by
PAUL SIMON

Take Me to the Mardi Gras

Words and Music by
PAUL SIMON

Come on, Take Me To The Mar - di Gras ___ where the peo - ple sing and

play, _____ Where the danc - ing is e - lite and there's

You can min-gle in the street, You can jin-gle to the beat of the jel-ly roll.

No chord

Tum-ba, tum-ba, tum-ba, Mar-di Gras,

Tum-ba, tum-ba, tum-ba day,_____ Mm_____

_____ Mm_____

Fifty Ways to Leave Your Lover

Words and Music by
PAUL SIMON

76

Hop on the bus, Gus; you don't need to dis-cuss____ much;____

____ just drop off the key, Lee, and get your-self free.

Slip out the free.

free.

Something So Right

Words and Music by
PAUL SIMON

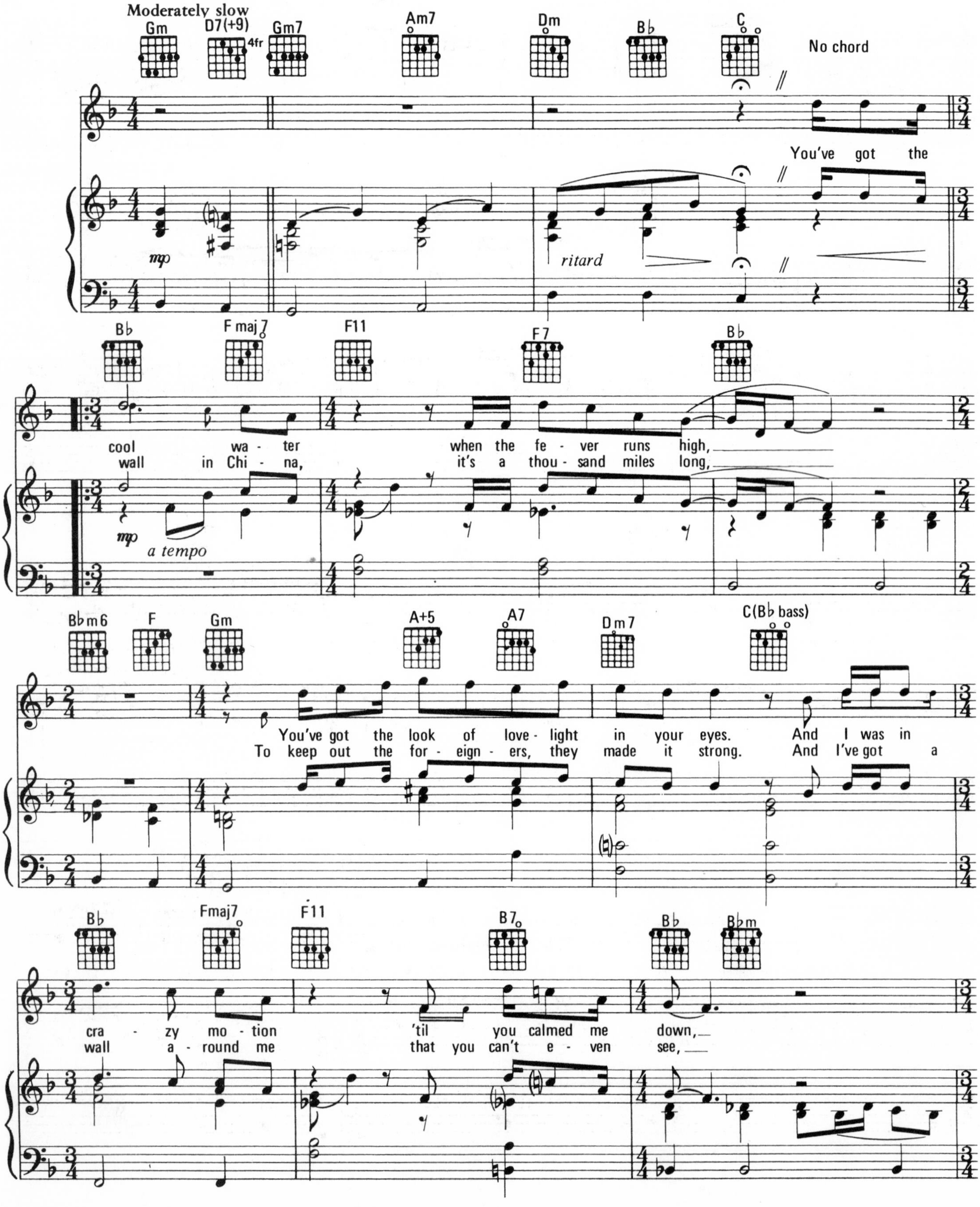

I Do It for Your Love

Words and Music by
PAUL SIMON

American Tune

Words and Music by
PAUL SIMON

Moderately slow

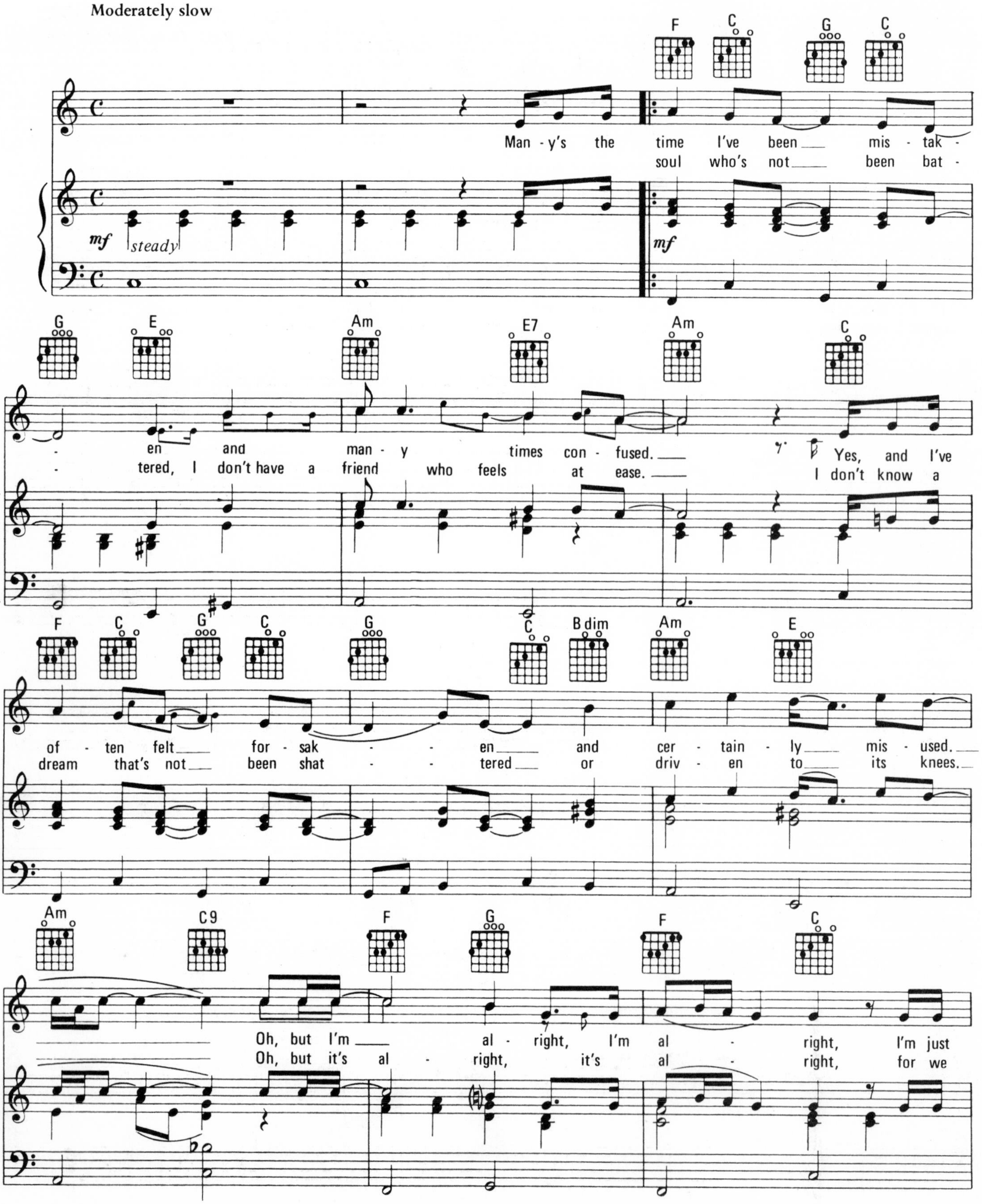

Man - y's the time I've been___ mis - tak -
soul who's not___ been bat -

mf steady

mf

- en and man - y times con - fused.___ Yes, and I've
- tered, I don't have a friend who feels at ease.___ I don't know a

of - ten felt___ for - sak - en___ and cer - tain - ly___ mis - used.___
dream that's not___ been shat - tered___ or driv - en to___ its knees.___

Oh, but I'm___ al - right, I'm al - right, I'm just
Oh, but it's al - right, it's al - right, for we

Kodachrome

Words and Music by
PAUL SIMON

With a moving beat

Verse 1.

F   Fmaj7   F7   F7+9

1. When I think back _____ on all _____ the crap _____ I learned in high _____

Bb   Gm

___ school,   It's a won - der

*"KODACHROME" is a registered trademark for color film.

And brought them all to-geth-er for one

night,   I know they'd nev - er match my

sweet im-ag-i-na-tion,___

And ev-'ry-thing looks worse in black and white. Ko-da-

D.S. al Fine 𝄋

Loves Me Like A Rock

Words and Music by
PAUL SIMON

Rock.   She rocks me like the rock of a - ges and loves__

__ me.__   She love me, love me, love me, love me.__

3. And if I was the Pres - i - dent, (Was_____ the Pres - i -

dent.) the min - ute the Con - gress call my name. (Was_____ the Pres - i -